GATOR DAD

Written and illustrated by

Brian Lies

HOUGHTON MIFFLIN HARCOURT

BOSTON   NEW YORK

Copyright © 2016 by Brian Lies

www.hmhco.com

The text of this book is set in Clarendon.
The illustrations were created with acrylic paint on Strathmore paper.

ISBN 978-0-544-53433-9

Manufactured in China
SCP 10 9 8 7 6 5 4 3 2 1

4500574691

Come on—

let's go!

Let's squeeze the day.

First we'll need some energy,

a treat to give us strength.

If something in the fridge has gone bad

. . . I'll let *you* smell it, too.

Next, we'll run some errands

before we wander out into the wild.

I'll help you try to touch the moon

More!

More!

More!

. . . and you'll probably need to rest.

I'll be your raft on a sea of grass,

a tree for you to climb.

I might even agree to do something

With nothing left to do,
we'll splash home
for a change.

We'll flop on the sofa, stay put for a while.

the
house

APART!

We'll see what it's like being someone else,

. . . and you can step on my toes.

After dinner, we'll rinse
away
the
day.

I may not be able to quiet the storm, but . . .

here in my arms you'll be safe and warm.

I'll be the robot you steer to your bed.

One more story,

one last squeeze.

Let's squeeze tomorrow, too.